名家经典双语绘本系列
Bilingual Picture Books of Classical Essays

风 筝

Kite

鲁 迅 / 文　张大军 / 图　王池英 / 译
Written by Lu Xun　Painted by Zhang Dajun
Translated by Wang Chiying

新世界出版社
NEW WORLD PRESS

北京的冬季，地上还有积雪，灰黑色的秃树枝丫叉于晴朗的天空中，而远处有一二风筝浮动，在我是一种惊异和悲哀。

One or two kites floating in the distance and leafless dark grey trees branching out and thrusting up into the clear blue sky – this bleak winter landscape of Peking gives me a stunning sense of sorrow.

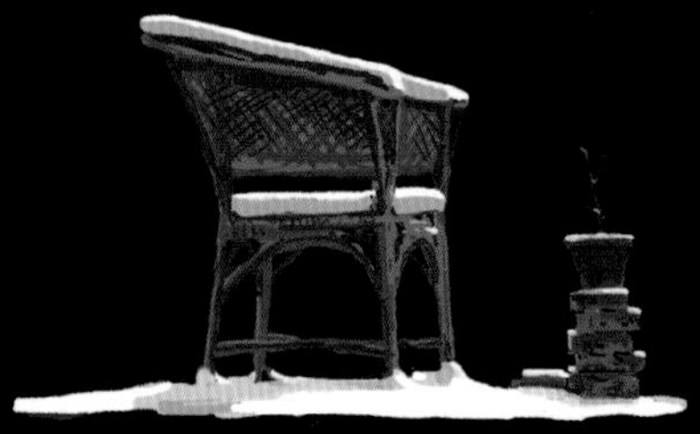

故乡的风筝时节，是春二月，倘听到沙沙的风轮声，仰头便能看见一个淡墨色的蟹风筝或嫩蓝色的蜈蚣风筝。还有寂寞的瓦片风筝，没有风轮，又放得很低，伶仃地显出憔悴可怜的模样。但此时地上的杨柳已经发芽，早的山桃也多吐蕾，和孩子们的天上的点缀相照应，打成一片春日的温和。

The best time to fly kites in my hometown in southern China is February. If you hear the swishing sound of a wind wheel and look up, you may catch sight of a pale inky crab-kite or tender blue centipede-kite. Or you may see an isolated tile-kite with no wind wheel flying low and lonely and looking pathetically haggard. By now, spring is already around the corner. As the poplars and willows put out their shoots and most early season peach trees produce their flower buds, nature has already joined hands with the kids who adorn the sky with their artwork in creating the warmth and

我现在在哪里呢？四面都还是严冬的肃杀，而久经诀别的故乡的久经逝去的春天，却就在这天空中荡漾了。

Now, while I am still surrounded by the severity and barrenness of winter, the long-gone spring of my long-parted hometown is already drifting away in the sky above me.

但我是向来不爱放风筝的，不但不爱，并且嫌恶他，因为我以为这是没出息孩子所做的玩艺。

I never liked kite flying myself. In fact, I hated it, because I thought it was a game for idle kids only.

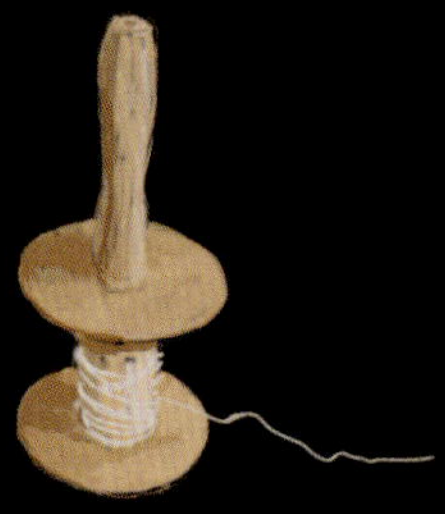

My sickly and emaciated younger brother who was around ten years old was quite different. He loved flying kites more than anything else, but he had no money to buy any, and even when he had one, I would not let him fly it. All he could do was to gaze raptly at the sky with his small mouth half open, sometimes for hours and hours.

He would give a scream of dismay when a crab-kite flying far away suddenly dropped. He would leap for joy when two entangled tile-kites got unwound and set free.

他的这些，在我看来都是笑柄，可鄙的。

And yet, in my eyes, all these excitements were just laughing stocks and grounds for contempt.

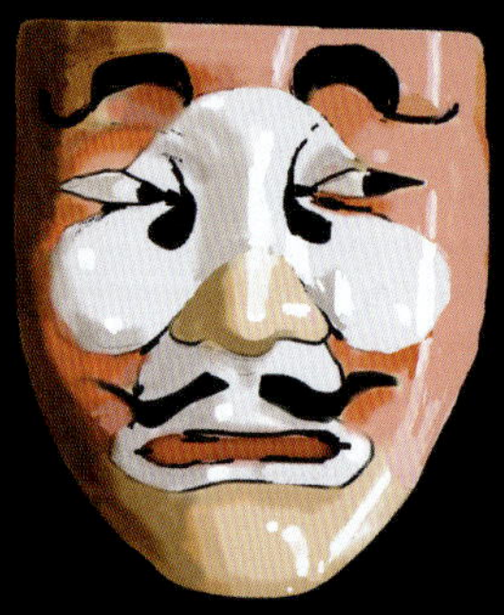

有一天，我忽然想起，似乎多日不很看见他了，但记得曾见他在后园拾枯竹。我恍然大悟似的，便跑向少有人去的一间堆积杂物的小屋去，推开门，果然就在尘封的杂物堆中发现了他。他向着大方凳，坐在小凳上；便很惊惶地站了起来，失了色瑟缩着。大方凳旁靠着一个胡蝶风筝的竹骨，还没有糊上纸，凳上是一对做眼睛用的小风轮，正用红纸条装饰着，将要完工了。

One day it suddenly occurred to me that it had been quite a few days since I last saw him, but I did remember seeing him pick up dried bamboo sticks in the backyard. Then it suddenly dawned on me what might have been going on. I ran to a deserted small storage room, pushed the door open, and sure enough, discovered him there in a dusty pile of debris. He was seated on a small footstool and facing a large square stool. At sight of me he rose to his feet shivering in fear and confusion, his face turning pale. Propped up against the large square stool was the bamboo framework of a butterfly-kite, which was yet to be pasted with paper. On top of the large stool lay two small wind wheels meant to be the butterfly's eyes, which were being draped with red paper ribbons and were about done.

我在破获秘密的满足中，又很愤怒他的瞒了我的眼睛，这样苦心孤诣地来偷做没出息孩子的玩艺。我即刻伸手抓断了胡蝶的一支翅骨，又将风轮掷在地下，踏扁了。论长幼，论力气，他是都敌不过我的，我当然得到完全的胜利，于是傲然走出，留他绝望地站在小屋里。后来他怎样，我不知道，也没有留心。

I was at once pleased to have busted his secret and furious to know that he had gone to such great lengths to hide from me and stealthily make such worthless stuff that only idle kids would make. I immediately grabbed the butterfly and broke one of the wing bones, threw the wind wheels on the floor and stamped on them. Naturally, my triumph was complete because he was no match for me in terms of age and strength. I swaggered out proudly and left him standing alone in despair in that small shed. I had no clue what happened to him afterwards, nor did I care at all.

然而我的惩罚终于轮到了，在我们离别得很久之后，我已经是中年。我不幸偶而看了一本外国的讲论儿童的书，才知道游戏是儿童最正当的行为，玩具是儿童的天使。于是二十年来毫不忆及的幼小时候对于精神的虐杀的这一幕，忽地在眼前展开，而我的心也仿佛同时变了铅块，很重很重的堕下去了。

但心又不竟堕下去而至于断绝，他只是很重很重地堕着，堕着。

However, my penalty finally came. After seeing him last a long time ago, I have since reached middle age. It was only after I had unfortunately and unintentionally read a foreign book on children that I learned that toys are children's angels and play is the most legitimate behavior of children. All of a sudden, the act of psychological abuse that I had committed 20 years before but had not recalled ever since came alive before my very eyes and seemed to have immediately turned my heart into a lump of lead that sank lower and lower, though never to the point of breaking.

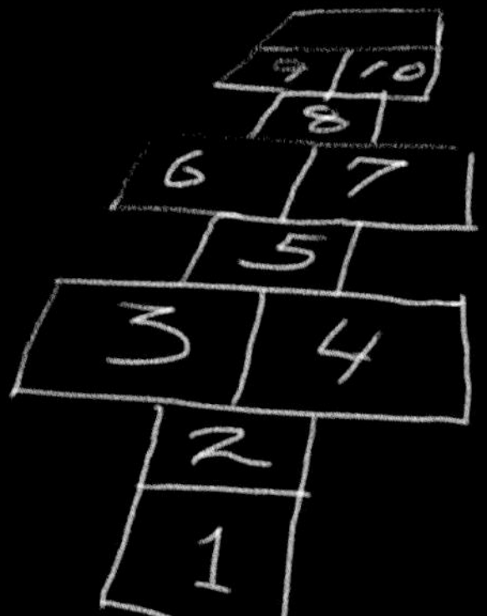

“我可是毫不怪你啊。”那么，我的心一定就轻松了，这确是一个可行的方法。

I knew how to make it up too – give him a kite, allow him to fly it, persuade him to do it, and even fly it with him. We would yell, run, and laugh. The pity is, he was already old enough to wear a moustache, just like me.

I also knew there was another way of making it up: ask him for forgiveness, and wait for him to say, “I don’t blame you at all.” That way, my heart would be immediately relieved of the burden of guilt.

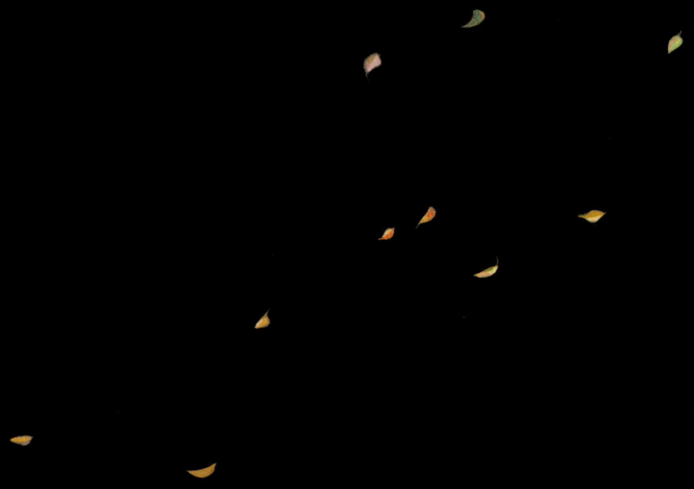

有一回，我们会面的时候，是脸上都已添刻了许多“生”的辛苦的条纹，而我的心很沉重。

The day we met again was when the “winters of life” had dug numerous “deep trenches” on our faces. My heart remained heavy laden.

我们渐渐谈起儿时的旧事来，我便叙述到这一节，自说少年时代的胡涂。“我可是毫不怪你呵。”我想，他要说了，我即刻便受了宽恕，我的心从此也宽松了罢。

“有过这样的事么？”他惊异地笑着说，就象旁听着别人的故事一样。他什么也不记得了。

As we started talking about anecdotes of our childhood, I mentioned the kite part and blamed myself for the follies of my youth. “I don’t blame you at all!” I thought he was going to say that and forgive me instantly, and my heart would be set free ever since.

“Did that really happen?” He asked in disbelief, smiling, as if he were hearing a story about someone else. He had clean forgotten about it!

全然忘却，毫无怨恨，又有什么宽恕之可言呢？无怨的恕，说谎罢了。

我还能希求什么呢？我的心只得沉重着。

现在，故乡的春天又在这异地的空中了，既给我久经逝去的儿时的回忆，而一并也带着无可把握的悲哀。我倒不如躲到肃杀的严冬中去罢，——但是，四面又明明是严冬，正给我非常的寒威和冷气。

Now, when the spring of my hometown is again up in the sky in this northern land, bringing back to me memories of my long-gone childhood together with its impalpable sadness, I feel I am better off hiding myself in the severity of winter. And yet, I know clearly I am already surrounded by the rigors of winter and feeling the brunt of their intensity and iciness.

一九二五年一月二十四日。

January 24, 1925

作者介绍：

鲁迅（1881—1936），中国文学家、思想家和革命家。原名周树人，字豫才，浙江绍兴人。

About the Author

Lu Xun (1881-1936), also known as Zhou Shuren, was born in Shaoxing, Zhejiang Province. He was a renowned Chinese writer, thinker, revolutionary and a leading figure of modern Chinese literature.

绘者介绍：

张大军，电影美术指导、绘本画家。中国戏曲学院毕业后一直从事美术指导工作至今。电影《冬至》获得第11届大学生电影节处女作奖。电影《红色康拜因》获得韩国釜山电影节影评人大奖。他也是“蒲蒲兰原创十年·绘本原画展”设计者，以童趣的设计、互动的体验为参观者津津乐道。他用绘本的方式，重新演绎了鲁迅名篇《风筝》，原画被鲁迅博物馆收藏。

About the Painter

Zhang Dajun is a film art director and picture book painter. He has engaged in art directing work ever since graduating from the National Academy of Chinese Theatre Arts.

With Mr. Zhang as art director, the film *The Coldest Day* won the Debut Award at the 11th Beijing College Student Film Festival and the film *The Red Awn* won the Critics' Award at the Busan International Film Festival.

He is also the designer of the "Poplar Ten Years: Original Painting Exhibition of Picture Books", which delighted visitors with its childlike designs and interactive experiences. Zhang's original paintings from this picture book have been collected by the Beijing Luxun Museum.

图书在版编目（CIP）数据

风筝：汉英对照 / 鲁迅著；张大军绘；王池英译
. -- 北京：新世界出版社，2021.12（2022.1 重印）
（名家经典双语绘本系列）
ISBN 978-7-5104-7363-0

Ⅰ. ①风… Ⅱ. ①鲁… ②张… ③王… Ⅲ. ①鲁迅散文－散文集－汉、英 Ⅳ. ①I210.4

中国版本图书馆CIP数据核字(2021)第227476号

风 筝（汉英对照）

作　　者：鲁　迅
绘　　者：张大军
翻　　译：王池英
责任编辑：孔德芳
英文审定：韩清月
装帧设计：贺玉婷
责任印制：王宝根　苏爱玲
出　　版：新世界出版社
网　　址：http://www.nwp.com.cn
社　　址：北京西城区百万庄大街24号（100037）
发 行 部：(010)6899 5968（电话）(010)6899 0635（电话）
总 编 室：(010)6899 5424（电话）(010)6832 6679（传真）
版 权 部：+8610 6899 6306（电话）nwpcd@sina.com（电邮）
印　　刷：小森印刷（北京）有限公司
经　　销：新华书店
开　　本：787mm × 1092mm　1/12　　尺寸：230mm × 230mm
字　　数：50千字　　印张：3
版　　次：2021年12月第1版　2022年1月第2次印刷
书　　号：ISBN 978-7-5104-7363-0
定　　价：52.80元

声明：本书文字参照《野草》（人民文学出版社，1973年3月第1版）。
为了尊重鲁迅先生的原作，在文字方面未作修正和规范，请读者理解。